The Berry Fairies of Alaska

ISBN No. 978-0-9816592-0-6

©2008 Teresa Ascone

First Edition ~ November 2008.

This book would not have been created without the the patience, love and support of my family: Mike and Michael Ascone. I also counted on the invaluable assistance of many wonderful friends. I especially express appreciation to the following people: Ann Chandonnet, Libby Roderick, Karen Sobolesky, Terri Storter, Jana Hayenga, Yana and Charlotte Smith, Janie Taylor, Barb Marsh, Peggy Ammann, Paula Easley, Colette LaRose, Laurie Boom, Mary Humphrey, Doug Lindstrand, Verna Pratt, Denise Statz, Bonnie Jack, Dawn Brunke, all the folks at Taku Graphics, and the Turbo Group: especially Diane S., Jan C., Susan M.,Susan H., Jane G., Ginny deV., and Vonni C. My little Jack Russell Terrier, Jackson, who is no longer with us, was the basis for the character of the paper wasp, Grimlet, who appears in the story, *"Lizzie Scarlet: A Tale of Envy."*

Published by

Alaskan Portfolio • PO Box 877706 • Wasilla, AK 99687
907-357-7622 • teresaascone@yahoo.com
www.berryfairies.net

Printed in Korea. Printing and binding through Aipex.com, Seattle, Washington

Front cover illustration portrays blueberry fairies Ellen and Azuria offering berries to a young moose.

Table of Contents

VENTURE YE NOW
INTO THE MYSTERIOUS AND MAGICAL
REALM OF FAERIE ~
THE WORLD OF THE

BERRY FAIRIES

OF ALASKA

PROLOGUE

In which
the Alaska Berry Fairy
Realm
is introduced –
their habitat, appearance,
purpose and ways.

S ometimes called *The Great Land*, Alaska is filled with many animals such as bear, moose, eagles, owls and geese.

People live there too, of course — and so do the
ALASKA BERRY FAIRIES!
Berry fairies exist worldwide, but this book is about the ones in Alaska. These magical folk are seldom seen by people, but they are always around, caring for the wonderful wild berries in this far northern land.

2

Alaska berry fairies belong to clans that care for their particular berry. The berry fairy clans are separated into two categories.

The GLAYIN berry fairies, who oversee poisonous or medicinal fruit like devil's club or snowberries, are more serious than the carefree and joyful DEEYIN, who watch over the delicious edible ones such as blueberries, salmonberries or cranberries.

Berry fairies are always of the female gender. They are six to eight inches tall — just the right size to perch on a human hand, although one never would.

Blueberry fairy Azuria, at left, is the daughter of Sehra, below.

Cranberry fairy Frammie, shown here with Dot, her ayonatta, is fascinated with gadgets. She turns discarded computers and other trezoran discoveries into berry fairy tools. This old cell phone, a recent find, is now a cranberry crop monitor powered by soil and root energy and a bit of berry fairy magic.

Merris, a salmonberry fairy (nicknamed Merri) is a smart redhead with a big personality. She sometimes gets into mischief, but only while searching for fun. She loves to dance and is seen frolicking here with Perriwink, her butterfly ayonatta (the purple one by her right hand) and other butterfly friends.

BERRY FAIRY WINGS

Alaska berry fairies can fly from a standing or crouching position. They have a denser network of wing veins than berry fairies in warmer climates. In summer, when the sun shines for many hours a day (Alaska is sometimes called *The Land of the Midnight Sun*), their wings absorb and store light. This stored light creates a glow that helps them see during the dark winter hours.

WING DEVELOPMENT

Baby to Toddler: Wings start as nubs and grow swiftly. Internal ribbing appears as a dot pattern. The berry fairy cannot fly until middle childhood (5-7 years old by human reckoning.)

Late Youth - Adulthood: Ribbing becomes more visible, and wings gain strength and flexibility. There are many variations of color and brilliance, which can change with the fairy's mood.

Elder Wings - Age 100 and up: Colors soften. Vertical stance relaxes into graceful curves. Ribbing thins slightly but wings remain strong.

BERRY FAIRY FASHION

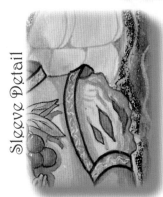

Sleeve Detail

Dance Frock

Berry fairies love pretty clothes. Trousers suits are the usual attire for hard work, sports, and long flights. For special occasions they like fancy sleeves and on warm days, sleeveless blouses are popular. One might think their love of fashion would mean they have hundreds of different outfits. Nothing could be further from the truth. They have the right clothes for every event, but none waste away in the closet unworn. Old clothes are deposited in a central area, carefully taken apart and re-used until the material is completely worn out.

ALASKA BERRY FAIRY SHOON*

✦ SHOES

delight the Alaska berry fairy:

Mukluks ✦ Lace ups ✦ Dance pumps ✦ Loopy sandals
✦ Waterproof "break up" boots for muddy Alaska spring times ✦

All types of comfortable and fashionable footwear line their shoe closets (flip-flops are seldom worn because they can come off during flight).

*Shoon: an old-fashioned word for shoes

ALASKA BERRY FAIRY MAGIC

Berry fairy magic is practiced with bracelets known as **KONJORS**. Gold nuggets found in Alaska streams and bright beads of berry juice (hardened and faceted in a secret process) make up the designs.

However, every power has its price — overuse of magic wastes energy and causes premature aging. The sad story of Jasill is told to youngsters in Berry Fairy Seminary. She was a bearberry fairy nicknamed Sillie, which might have been her problem because she developed silly habits. She enjoyed many compliments on her clear complexion, luminous eyes, and shiny hair. One day, gazing into the looking glass, she saw a tiny laugh line which caused her great dismay. She began to use her magic to erase every dimple, crease or spot from her face. Her anxious eyes looked for her reflection everywhere. Whether mirrored in a dewdrop or mud puddle, her own face fascinated her. She grew lazy, hardly ever thought of her berries and neglected them; other bearberry fairies had to take over her duties. Her face began to look like a china doll's — beautiful, but rigid and unmoving. Suddenly one day she died, still perfectly formed yet fatally fragile — the misuse of her magic had caused a wasting away of her spirit until there was nothing left but a lovely shell.

Silly indeed!

In matters concerning their crops, the berry fairies have authority over most animals. Here, a blueberry fairy holds serious counsel with a Kodiak bear for foraging too enthusiastically in the blueberry fields. RODDEELS, or ravens, are berry fairy allies and protect them from predators such as the KRILLKLAWS, known as magpies in the English language.

8

SOUTHCENTRAL ALASKA

Matanuska Valley

Anchorage

Kenai Peninsula

Kodiak Island

©ASCONE

T he main Alaska berry fairy settlement is located in Southcentral Alaska, which includes the Matanuska Valley, the Kenai Peninsula, Cook Inlet and Alaska's largest city, Anchorage. Berry fairy strongholds thrive there in secret places: perched on islands, deeply tunneled under old beaver dams, and hidden beneath tree roots.

9

DWELLARIES

door detail

window

The dwellary extends up along the tree roots and under the rocks

Alaska berry fairy homes are called DWELLARIES. Berry fairies often take up residence in burrows or caves previously occupied by other forest creatures — even abandoned birds' nests if they can be made roomy enough for the fairy's needs. Remodeling is always necessary and is accomplished by FORESTFOLKE kin.

ALASKA BERRY FAIRY GOVERNMENT

Queen Prasidea Silverbirch, who lives in southcentral Alaska, oversees all the Alaska clans and with the ELDEERA — the elders — she considers and settles major disputes such as berry field boundary questions or violations of the SACRE NINYIN, the Nine Sacred Principles.

Next in order of authority are the FAE-REJENTS: leaders of each clan. Fae-rejency is passed down from mother to daughter.

Royal Insignia

Her Royal Majesty, Queen Prasidea, was born into the Snowberry Fairy Clan. Upon taking royal office, she swore loyalty to all berry fairies and vowed never to favor any particular clan.

BERRY FAIRY AYONATTAS

The berry fairies have lifelong best friends in the insect world. In berry fairy language they are known as AYONATTAS. Favorites of Alaska berry fairies are dragonflies, hornets, butterflies and ladybugs (The official Alaska insect is the dragonfly, not the mosquito as many suppose).

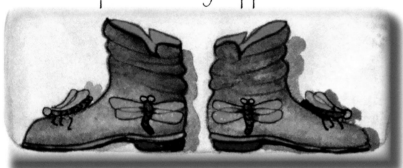

Ayonatta Decoration on Boots

The ayonattas assist their fairies in every way possible. They are kind, encouraging — and skilled at hairstyling. They work for many hours in the berry fields with their fairy mistresses and never complain.

Young ayonattas are sworn to their berry fairies using an ancient magic spell, *"Sacrenoptera Transformis!"* which gives them certain magic powers, long life and the ability to survive the long Alaska winters. After vowing eternal devotion and loyalty, ayonattas are given a tiny gold ring to wear on their first left leg. This signifies their new status in the insect world — for they, as the chosen ones of the berry fairies, are considered the royalty of their race.

ALASKA BERRY FAIRY INDUSTRY

Alaska berry fairies are among the most creative of all the fairy races. They make numerous products from their berries, and also recycle items like shed moose antlers. Alaska berry fairy soap, made from a secret recipe, is famous throughout the fairy realms. Complexion Bliss is a favorite from Alaska to New Zealand.

Alaska Berry Fairy Blueberry Soap

Lip Bliss, considered by the fairies as the best lip moisturizer in the world, protects them during cold Alaska winters and dry summer days.

When Alaska berry fairies reach retirement, between 100 and 120 years of age, they become members of the eldeera — the elders — and are invited to live in a cozy apartment located on

BERRY FAIRY LIBRARY
AND
DAY SPA

VEGETABLE
GARDENS

AERIAL VIEW
FOR BERRY FAIRIES
& FORESTFOLKE

ZEER
MEDITEE

DEEYIN
HOUSE

THE THREE WATERFALLS

CRYSTAL POOL
OF PURITY

GLAYIN HOUSE

BONHAM
MOUNTAINS

FORESTFOLK
BEACH

CLAY DIG

BOREAL RO

the Isle of Aeradeet, located somewhere in Cook Inlet. Also on the island is The Crystal Pool of Purity, a clear, shallow lake five inches deep with a sandy bottom.

FORESTFOLKE POTTERY AND
QUONSET DWELLARY

BONJJAIN
MOUNTAINS

SPORTS
AND DANCE ARENA

"THE ROUND HOUSE"
ELDEERA APARTMENT
DWELLARY

The
Isle of
Aeradeet

BERRY FAIRY
SEMINARY

ZELL
MEDITEE

RODDEEL
PEAK

PONTENDARK
BRIDGE

MIKALLIST
MESA

ROZLANDIS
ISLAND

Two spacious buildings serve as dormitories for visiting fairies: Deeyin House and Glayin House. There are two labyrinths for meditation: Zell Meditee for flying, which features a deck atop the spiral-trimmed spruce tree, and Zeer Meditee for walking. Aeradeet is protected by INVONDEE, a magic mist that conceals the island from shiltayen eyes.

It is filled by three waterfalls, one of which is a natural hot spring that keeps the pool a comfortable 80 degrees year round.

BERRY FAIRIES AND HUMAN BEINGS

Berry fairies can wield secret power over the SHILTAYEN — their word for human beings. Shiltayen "luck," coincidence and inspiration sometimes come from fairy influence. They are too busy with the care and welfare of their berries to pay much interest; however, since fashion is an area of berry fairy fascination, they sometimes secretly take a shiltayen clothing expert under their wing. Some of the most admired designers in history owe their success to fairy spells. But their influence is not always a plus; berry fairy humor can result in shiltayen foolishness.

For instance, the stiff hoop skirts of the 1800s were a result of berry fairy fashion mischief. The 1960s trend of extra wide bell bottom trousers (pictured) is known, in fairy lore, to have been a hilarious prank played upon the shiltayen by the berry fairies.

Architects can occasionally fall under their control as well. A few of the strangest-looking structures in Alaska originated from architects who, wrapped in daydreams merrily spun by the berry fairies, designed buildings that puzzle or dismay the town residents.

Ever thrifty and creative, the berry fairies and their friends, the FORESTFOLKE, find useful items in the TREZORANS, which the shiltayen call dumps or landfills.

SAKRE NINYIN

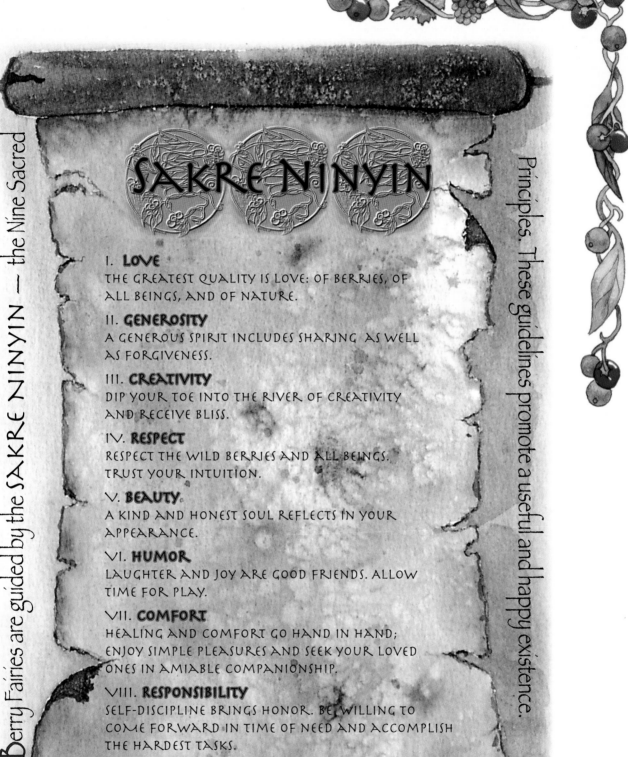

I. LOVE
THE GREATEST QUALITY IS LOVE: OF BERRIES, OF ALL BEINGS, AND OF NATURE.

II. GENEROSITY
A GENEROUS SPIRIT INCLUDES SHARING AS WELL AS FORGIVENESS.

III. CREATIVITY
DIP YOUR TOE INTO THE RIVER OF CREATIVITY AND RECEIVE BLISS.

IV. RESPECT
RESPECT THE WILD BERRIES AND ALL BEINGS. TRUST YOUR INTUITION.

V. BEAUTY
A KIND AND HONEST SOUL REFLECTS IN YOUR APPEARANCE.

VI. HUMOR
LAUGHTER AND JOY ARE GOOD FRIENDS. ALLOW TIME FOR PLAY.

VII. COMFORT
HEALING AND COMFORT GO HAND IN HAND; ENJOY SIMPLE PLEASURES AND SEEK YOUR LOVED ONES IN AMIABLE COMPANIONSHIP.

VIII. RESPONSIBILITY
SELF-DISCIPLINE BRINGS HONOR. BE WILLING TO COME FORWARD IN TIME OF NEED AND ACCOMPLISH THE HARDEST TASKS.

IX. COURAGE
STEP THROUGH THE FEARFUL TIMES. DEFEND AND PROTECT WHAT IS DEAR TO YOU. KEEP LOYALTY, EVEN IN THE DARKEST HOUR, TO YOUR OWN BELIEFS.

(C)ASCONE

16

A DAY IN THE LIFE OF AN ALASKA BERRY FAIRY

She rises early in active berry seasons: spring, summer and fall. A wake-up alarm is not needed since her fairy instinct awakens her at the right time.

Two hearty meals a day plus an evening snack keep her lively. During breakfast — porridge with berries or sourdough pancakes with plenty of butter and berry syrup, she reads the *Alaska Berry Fairy Daily Gazette*. If she expects a hard day she will add a devil's club infusion to her berry tea.

After breakfast she heads to her work day which is longer in summer due to the extended daylight hours. The season dictates her tasks, which could include planting, leaf dusting, thinning, directing pollination and weeding (most weeds are edible, so berry fairies consider them a kind of harvest). Tasting, testing and preserving happen late in the season. Before snowfall, she mulches the fields with fallen leaves.

At midday the fairy is eager for a lunch of vegetables, fresh fish and mixed berry compote. Chocolate is usually served, both for its antioxidant value and as a tasty energy boost. A goblet of berry shrub completes the meal. Children frolic while the fairy naps before afternoon work.

ForestFolke prepare a buffet snack to graze upon in the later hours. The fairy relaxes by painting, playing with children, or chatting with friends over a board game or cards. She usually takes a bath and performs her JANEERA exercise and meditation before bedtime in the privacy of her BOREAL, a chamber located within the dwellary.

This routine continues for four days, followed by three days of recreation or travel. She often flies to Aeradeet for sports, songfests and dances.

Thus does the Alaska berry fairy spend her day, enjoying life and rejoicing in her mission of ensuring berry welfare and abundance.

AND SO . . .
The Alaska berry fairy clans
protect and cultivate
their beloved wild berries.
They continue to thrive
through the ages,
in power, yet in secret . . .
enriching the Great Land
with delicious berries to eat,
and medicinal ones to cure
the ills of all folk.

18

ALASKA BERRY FAIRY MYSTIQUE

As day slips into twilight and stars shine on the dell,
Imagination takes flight — and fairies cast their spell.

Observant folk can glimpse them as they frolic in the night
Tending to their berries in the pale moonlight.

Berry fairies always know — though, like daisies, never tell
The secret caves and hideouts where their fairy sisters dwell.

If you listen closely, on a calm Alaska dawn
You can hear their laughter for a moment — then they're gone.

Flown away to hide from shiltayen curious eyes.
We could never catch them as they whisk into the skies.

Deeyin and Glayin, serious or sweet,
Both kinds of berry fairies in the forest gladly meet —

To cultivate their berries so all creatures on the Earth
Can treasure Nature's bounty from Kotzebue to Perth.

I'd like to be a fairy, playing in the sun —
Flying loop-the-loops with friends when berry work is done.

Enjoy their precious berries, juicy, ripe and sweet;
But be careful not to squash them beneath your careless feet.

The sisters would be saddened to know this tragedy —
To waste their priceless treasures
'stead of picking them, you see.

So be sure, when strolling in the woods,
where all those berries lay —
to honor and respect their work
the berry fairy way.

19

Sehra Twinkle's Love Story

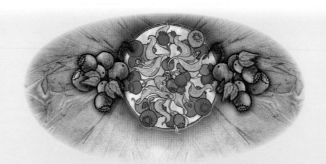

Sehra Falls in Love

At the tender age of thirty-seven, at an evening picnic under the stars in the Matanuska Valley, Sehra Twinkle fell in love. Although her mother, Brittallo, at first objected on the grounds that she was too young, Sehra would not be denied her wish; she was smitten with John Wilderbranche, and he with her. Sehra, being a willful berry fairy and the newly ascended fae-rejent leader of the Blueberry Clan, had her mind made up. Marry John Wilderbranche she would.

Not that Sehra's family disapproved of John — far from it. An eligible Forestfolke bachelor eyed by many a love-struck berry fairy, he was considered most worthy of Sehra. The venerable and wealthy Wilderbranche Clan was well respected. Besides, John's mother, Anneen, was Brittallo's third cousin three times removed so it was not as if they were complete strangers, although they lived in different parts of the country.

The whirlwind courtship was followed by a typical berry fairy long engagement. Brittallo Twinkle's objections melted away when, upon visiting Anneen Wilderbranche's luxurious, moss-covered estate hidden in the Denali foothills, she was reminded of the ancient nobility of the clan. With the backing of the Wilderbranches, her daughter would want for nothing. Sehra had not only made a classic love match, but one that would be secure and stable. John's obvious adoration of Sehra was the tipping point towards Brittallo's complete approval of the marriage.

Thus, the Twinkle clan started planning the ceremony. The marriage of a clan fae-rejent was equal in importance to a shiltayen royal coronation; it would take years of preparation.

John searched high and low for just the right engagement gift for his fiancée. As he searched, he recalled their first meeting, and how the thunderbolt of love had struck them both.

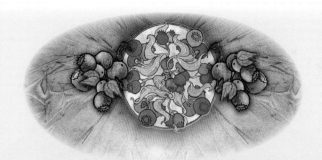

He, a stout, hearty youth of forty-two, had planned a fishing trip. The Sticklebacks were swarming in the lakes of the Kenai Peninsula, and his mother's fish larder was nearly empty.

An expert sportsman, he relished a day of fishing. Naturally, when his mother announced the big picnic planned for that day at ForestFolke Beach, John protested, "Mother, not this time. The fish are running. I'm packed and ready to go."

But his mother insisted, "John, I would much rather you come to the picnic. We need help setting up umbrellas, tables and benches." John sighed. As ever, it was difficult to deny his mother's request. Little did he know that soon he would meet the berry fairy of his dreams.

A Picnic at ForestFolke Beach

He first laid eyes on the fair Sehra as she was bustling about carrying baskets of food, her dragonfly ayonatta, Lissabelle, at her side. All thoughts of fishing flew from his brain. Who was this beautiful creature? Sehra caught sight of him glancing her way. "What a handsome lad," she thought.

As the picnic got underway, John deftly maneuvered next to Sehra and they were soon engaged in lively conversation. They spent the entire day together, and their mutual attraction did not go unnoticed. John's mother managed to catch his eye and smile her approval.

A Special Night

As the September dusk crept into darkness and the campfires glowed orange against sand and sky, Sehra and John filled their cups with salmonberry punch and sat a distance away from the others. As the gazed up at the starry sky, John gathered his courage and took her hand. Sehra's heart beat fast, and she felt a thrill of happiness.

"Look! The stars are bright tonight," said Sehra. "There's the Great Berry constellation, and we can see Konjor and the Ayonatta grouping." John remained silent; he was entranced by other stars — the ones shining in Sehra's warm, brown eyes.

Feeling a bit self-conscious, Sehra began to chatter about the ancient berry fairy legend of the big round, blue-green berry called Earth and the creation of the berry fairies. John had heard it many times, but he listened, fascinated by the sound of her voice.

Sehra pointed to a group of stars. "John, did you know that the Great Berry constellation symbolizes the birth of berries?" She began to relate the legend. "At the beginning of time, there was only one berry bush on Earth. No one knew where it came from, but it began to grow here in the fertile Matanuska Valley. It needed care and nurturing, so we berry fairies came into being to guard it and ensure its survival. Our race named the bush and its fruit the Great Berry."

John listened intently, looking into Sehra's eyes. Encouraged, she went on. "The Great Berry's vines and leaves spread over vast areas. Thanks to our faithful care, its yield increased. Ripe, sweet and bursting with juice, the yield from the first Great Berry fed the multitudes."

"Our ancestors looked at their work and declared it wonderful. They had faith that the Great Berry could bear fruit of different kinds, and began experimentation and cross-pollination with other species of plants, which resulted in the many different berries of today."

Sehra paused for breath. In the silence, John said softly, "Please, go on."

She blushed and continued, "A natural division of labor occurred within our race as the berries multiplied: our ancestors named the ones who cared for the poisonous, medicinal berries the Glayin, and those who watched over edible berries were declared the Deeyin."

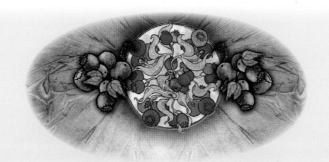

Sehra paused again in her story and took a sip of punch. She glanced at John and laughed softly. "Now, when you look at the stars and see the Great Berry constellation, you'll always remember the story and this night."

John, his natural charm coming into play, whispered, "I will, indeed, always remember this night, not just for your fascinating story but for another, more personal reason." Sehra's face flushed with pleasure. They gazed up, and suddenly a bright shooting star arced across the darkness. "Oh, Sehra, look!" John declared. "Make a wish!"

Engaged!

They held hands, closed their eyes, and each made a wish. Two minds on a single thought: I am in love. I wish we could be together forever! Sehra quickly cautioned, "We can't tell, or it won't come true." They gazed at one another and knew they were sweethearts.

A man of action, John wanted to impress this beautiful berry fairy. Always good at shiltayen-style Haiku poetry, he thought for a moment and created two Haiku. He recited the first one in a tender baritone:

> *I sing your praises,*
> *Wingêd girl of golden hair—*
> *You, who own my heart!*

Sehra's brown eyes sparkled and she smiled, which emboldened John to declare his intentions with a poetic proposal of marriage:

> *Steadfast courage, love,*
> *Everlasting devotion—*
> *These I offer you.*

John leaned towards her and planted a kiss upon her cheek. Sehra, deeply impressed, nodded her answer, "Yes, John, I will marry you. I will be your wife." Thus, they were officially engaged.

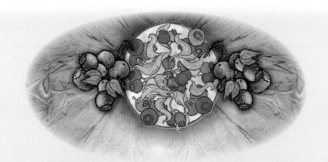

The Wedding Gifts

After much thought, John chose as Sehra's engagement gift a set of berry fairy story volumes, the deluxe one published by Berry Fairy Press. Bound in purple mushroom suede with her name embossed in gold leaf on the spines, it was, indeed, a fine present. Of course, the legend of the Great Berry was included to mark the day of their meeting.

Next, he set his mind to finding a wedding gift for his bride-to-be. John decided on a set of dishware crafted by his own hands. Since berry fairies and ForestFolke live a long time, it would be a fifty place set.

His first task was to find exactly the right raw material. Climbing higher than anyone had before, he discovered a deposit of toasty brown clay nestled high in the Bonjjain Mountains, on the Isle of Aeradeet. It was just the color of Sehra's eyes.

It was a dangerous climb but John was agile and fearless. He dug the clay and brought it, bit by bit, to the quonset pottery near ForestFolke Beach.

Crouched over his pottery wheel during the long somnin winters, John created an exquisite set of earthenware. He made soup tureens, salad plates, dinner plates, gravy boats, fiddlehead fern platters — every kind of dish they might need. There would be none other like it in the world.

Sehra liked herbal tea, so he designed delicate teacups with graceful handles. Pancake platters with dimples for holding birch tree syrup and tall tumblers for berry juice graced his pottery shelves.

Not content with food dishes, he made other vessels as well. Tiny saucers to cradle luxuriant bars of blueberry soap and stately vases with fluted rims came from his wheel.

He decorated the dishes with blueberry designs then finished them with a transparent glaze. Pleased with the results of his labor, he carefully packed the

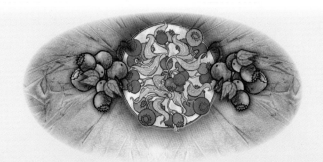

earthenware in Fireweed fluff until the wedding.

Meanwhile, Sehra prepared to make John's wedding present. She wanted something very special for him. It must be handmade, knitted with soft yarn spun from rakneet threads found on the rocky cliffs along Turnagain Arm. Spun by the orb weaver spiders that live among the cliffs, it was silky but durable enough to survive the wind and storms from the tidal area, and lightweight so that the gossamer webs could catch the spiders' insect prey. Berry fairies gathered it when the webbing had been abandoned so as not to interfere with the orb weaver's survival.

An Unexpected Peril

One sunny morning, Sehra and her dragonfly companion Lissabelle set out with a basket to collect the rakneet. "Mother, we're leaving now and should be gone all day," said Sehra.

Her mother, who was preparing packets of berries for the roddeels, the ravens, glanced up from her work. "Remember to be watchful for the krillklaws, Sehra," she cautioned, "and try not to stray very far from each other." Krillklaws, known to the shiltayen as magpies, considered the berry fairies delicious treats and ate them whenever they could catch them.

"And don't touch down on the tidal mud flats, you might get stuck!" Brittallo shouted as the two took off.

"Don't worry, mother! We know what to do, and we'll be safe," Sehra replied. "She frets too much. We've heard all that a thousand times," she whispered to Lissabelle as they ascended into the south wind currents.

They arrived at the cliffs a half hour later. Lissabelle, whose job was to locate webs, found several promising bunches. The orb weaver spider usually takes her web down each morning, so any they found could be collected without concern. Sehra began to gather the material, which was sticky to the touch before

processing. Later, it would be soaked in blueberry essence, then dried, dyed and spun into the soft blue yarn so treasured by the blueberry fairies.

The two gradually strayed far apart as Lissabelle searched the rock crevices and Sehra collected the webs in her basket. As she worked high on the cliff, perched upside down on the edge of a boulder, a shadow passed over her and Sehra heard the sound of wings — bird wings.

The blueberry fairy felt a sudden chill of fear. A moment later, as the attack came from below in a flurry of black and white feathers, she had only a moment to cry out to Lissabelle, "Hide!" Krillklaws, two of them, came at her with beaks and talons. As a claw viciously ripped her jacket, Sehra knew she was in a fight for her life.

Berry fairy defense training and survival instinct took over as she protected herself, aiming powerful kicks and wing strikes at the birds, which were beaten back momentarily. Then they continued their attack, one of them snapping at her leg while the other struck a glancing blow to her head. Everything went dim as Sehra plummeted wings over heels towards the treacherous tidal flats below.

Rescue!

Tumbling through the sky, the semi-conscious fairy dimly heard sounds of the fight continuing. A second later, her stomach turned flip flops as she found herself scooped onto the broad, strong back of a roddeel. Lissabelle, her dragonfly ayonatta, clutched neck feathers as the raven's powerful, black wings bore them in a sweeping arc away from the quicksand-like mud.

The roddeels, trusted allies of the berry fairies, were heroes. It was a stroke of luck that two of them had been patrolling the cliffs when the attack occurred and had rushed to rescue Sehra and Lissabelle. The dragonfly, dashing to help her mistress, had been swept onto one roddeel's back as he maneuvered a daring plunge through the sky to Sehra's aid. The other roddeel made short

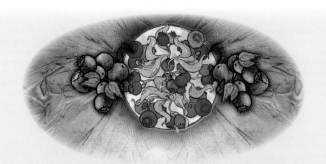

work of the two krillklaws and they swerved away in hasty retreat. He snatched up Sehra's basket of precious rakneet and swiftly caught up with his partner. The two ravens delivered Sehra and Lissabelle safely home.

News of the dramatic battle and rescue swept through the Matanuska Valley berry fairy settlement. John wept tears of relief when he heard of the narrow escape. The couple drew even closer as this threat to their future, averted by the heroism of their roddeel friends, hit home.

Sehra never again scoffed at her mother's cautions. The Twinkle clan expressed their gratitude for Sehra's safety with a celebration dinner. Her wedding gift for John, a handsome set of rakneet nightwear knitted from the webs collected with such unexpected peril, would hold great meaning for the couple and the entire Alaska Blueberry Fairy Clan.

The Wedding of the Season

Finally, John and Sehra were wed. Years of planning brought forth a bountiful wedding celebration. All manner of folk had sent RSVPs in the affirmative.

The Twinkles, knowing the historic significance of this event, spared no expense on the wedding decorations and nuptial feast. Every member of the family had houseguests to accommodate attendees from distant lands.

John's kin brought costly presents for the couple. The Wilderbranche family had made its fortune by panning and digging for gold, so most of their gifts were made from the precious metal. Fine goblets, sewing needles, shoe buckles, and flatware embossed with the Wilderbranche and Twinkle emblems — all were laid on the already groaning gift tables. For Sehra, a handsome berry basket woven of fine gold threads shone on its own display stand. John's gift from his father was a golden fishing rod with all the tackle to go with it. Rare imported teas and coffees were brought to stock the newlyweds' larder, along with smoked

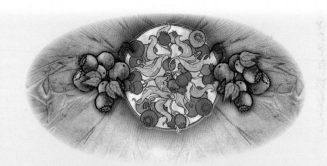

salmon and pickled Stickleback from his mother's kitchen. The couple would want for nothing.

As the wedding hour drew close, guests filed in excitedly, knowing that this would be the wedding of the season. It was an evening ceremony, drenched in romance. A canopy of lavender iris lace led up the walkway to the nuptial hall, which was draped in great swags of blue satin accented by the Blueberry Fairy Clan insignia. The glistening fabric mirrored the glow of a thousand pure white beeswax candles cradled in ornate brass holders — a generous gift from the bumblebees. Tiny white water lilies floated in cupped aspen leaves at the altar and in the corners of the hall.

The crowd gasped in awe as Sehra appeared in shimmering splendor, framed by the arched doorway. John, waiting nervously at the altar, gazed upon his bride like a love-struck schoolboy. His palms began to perspire. How exquisite she looked!

The amber candle flame halos reflected in her glistening bodice as she glided down the aisle. Her golden, blueberry jewel-studded fae-rejent tiara sparkled with the light of ten thousand stars.

Sehra's bridal ensemble was breathtaking. True to the berry fairy spirit of fashion, it fit perfectly. Her translucent wings trembled slightly behind a fingertip-length veil of snowflake lace. A separate length of lace veiled her face, forming a waterfall from her tiara to her shoulders. The princess-waist gown had a sweetheart neckline trimmed in slender gold threads worked into a chain of lovers' knots; the fitted bodice was encrusted with tiny mother-of-pearl chanteel.

From the pink-corded waistline a gathered silk skirt, lined in dusty rose netting, flowed to the floor and extended in a train held aloft by Lissabelle. Sehra's wildflower bouquet was accented by tiny crystal blueberries. Miniature ferns peeked out from the flowers here and there. Pale blue ribbons trailed from

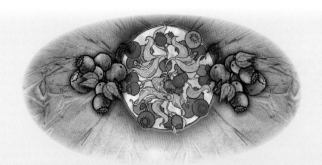

the bouquet. Her grandmother's tiny seed pearl earrings adorned her ears, and a matching single strand pearl choker encircled her neck. Wrapped around her left wrist was a heavy gold nugget double konjor, a gift from her parents. And her shoes! They were the most admired of all. Made by the queen's cobbler with sheets of 24K gold, the stylish pumps with tiny kitten heels were flawless. The toe of each shoe was covered in shiny silver blueberries.

John looked festive in his wedding suit: an Alaskan Tuxedo of green twill set off by a chunky gold nugget string tie clasp. Gold nugget buttons, heirlooms from the Wilderbranche treasure chamber, gleamed like sunlight, adding elegance to his appearance. His eyes shone with adoration for Sehra, and she thought he was the handsomest fellow she had ever seen.

As part of their vows, John swore allegiance to the Sakre Ninyin, the nine sacred berry fairy principles. Thus, the couple would be united in both love and the berry fairy belief system.

A Feast to Remember

Their rollicking party took place a week after the wedding and just before Renuvelle, the springtime berry fairy festival.

What a feast! Tiny grilled shrimp nestled on a bed of baby dandelion greens. Spring-fresh, tightly furled fiddlehead ferns were sautéed in creamy butter and drizzled with tart cranberry syrup. The guests devoured tray after tray of vegetables, and berry salads filled the tables. Dessert consisted of a six-tier wedding cake decorated with sugar blueberries and festooned with candied honey strands.

The music was a gift of the insects. Ladybugs and thumping beetles provided percussion and rhythm, while hornets and damselflies rubbed their wings together for the violin-like melodies. The guests danced for days.

At the height of the festivities, John presented his wedding gift. He declared, "My dearest bride, let these beautiful and sturdy vessels made from the Earth symbolize my eternal devotion and steadfast commitment to you."

Sehra was delighted, and, in keeping with blueberry fairy custom, served a wedding toast of blueberries topped with ice cream in the new berry bowls.

Sehra's gift to John, the suit of nightwear made from the Turnagain Arm rakneet collected on Sehra's now-famous adventure, was the subject of much admiration. Knitted in tiny stitches by the fairy and her devoted Lissabelle, it was indeed handsome. The lightweight stitch pattern was known for keeping husbands warm on cold nights, and cool on warm nights. Sehra had dyed it the exact color of ripe blueberries to complement his green hair.

Sehra and John set up a cozy dwellary sheltered beneath a large tree, close to her mother's somnin winter cabin on the Kenai Peninsula. A bay where herring swarmed was nearby, and a small waterfall flowed into a quiet stream bordered by wildflowers and berries.

Brown Eyes Turn Blue

One morning, many months later, John yawned, stretched, and leapt out of bed to begin his day. As his bride arose and threw the coverlet over the bed, she shot a loving glance at John and he gasped, "Oh, glorious day! Go, darling, and look into the mirror!"

Confused, Sehra darted into the bath chamber and glanced at her reflection. She also shrieked a cry of joy. Instead of her usual warm, brown orbs staring back at her, her eyes were as blue as luscious, ripe blueberries. Oh, glorious day indeed! Her blue eyes told her that she and John would soon be parents of a berry fairy.

Pregnancy instantly changes the color of a berry fairy's eyes. They turn blue when she is expecting a berry fairy and green if she is expecting a ForestFolke

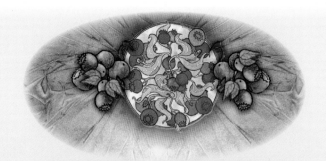

offspring — so John and Sehra knew they would be blessed with a girl fairy child. Fae-rejent Sehra felt especially blessed. Her daughter, if deemed worthy, would someday become the leader of her beloved Alaska Blueberry Fairy Clan.

The happy couple scheduled a large dinner party to include all the Wilderbranche and Twinkle kin. They revealed nothing about the impending birth, but merrily conspired to have Sehra greet each guest upon arrival; sharp-eyed kin would see her blue eyes and know the glad tidings.

Thrilled shouts echoed as both families realized their good fortune. Members of the Blueberry Fairy Clan were relieved in knowing that there would be a future Twinkle fae-rejent to continue their line of authority. The Wilderbranches would have a darling granddaughter to coddle, an unusual treat because most of their grandchildren so far had been boys.

After much thought and consultation with kin, the couple decided to name their baby girl Azuria Blue.

John Begins a Project

While awaiting her birth, John designed a suite of rooms for the baby. A cozy chamber would become her boreal, the retreat used by all berry fairies for the daily janeera meditation hour. It would be just large enough for a comfortable armchair, side table, and a mat for the exercise part of the janeera.

Another room would include a triple-decker bed for sleepovers. Suspended from the ceiling of the chamber, it was built of birch twigs, leaves, fragrant clover blossoms for springiness and Fireweed fluff for softness.

John wove moose hairs, the stiff ones shed from the back hump of the animal, under the mattresses for support webbing. Knitted spruce needle blankets, treated to remain aromatic, soft and pliable, were neatly folded over each bed. Crisp, white frost muslin coverlets finished the beds, and three tiny seashells, found on the rocky beach that faced the ocean near their dwellary,

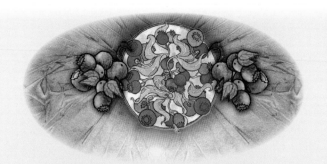

became nests for the berry fairies' ayonattas.

While on his weekly salvaging trip to the trezoran, John found a perfect piece of glass: half of a broken pickle jar. When buffed and properly trimmed, it would be the ideal curved pane for a bay window looking out on the stream.

Bookshelves lined the walls of baby Azuria's bedroom, along with gifts of artwork, tools and musical instruments — all received at berry fairy baby showers. A split willow twig desk sat in the corner. Two smaller rooms would hold clothing, shoes and jewelry, and a locked cabinet would eventually protect her magic konjors.

The fun-loving expectant father also remembered a set of three plastic pocket protectors previously salvaged at the trezoran. With some minor alterations, they would make ideal snow sleds for skimming over the hills near Halibut Cove.

Azuria Blue

Finally, preparations were complete for the birth. On the 25th day of August, after a pregnancy of 36 months, John and Sehra became the proud parents of Azuria Blue. As they counted their precious daughter's fingers, toes, and wing nubs, Sehra and John were overjoyed with their good fortune.

And so Azuria Blue Twinkle, a joyful girl with eyes the color of ripe pinecones and hair of gold, enjoyed a typical fairy childhood. Sehra resolved to start her early on the berry fairy mission; as a toddler, the girl mastered little tasks such as leaf dusting and berry picking.

Sehra took Azuria flying as soon as she could cling tightly to her mother's foot, and the little fairy loved the feeling of soaring over the treetops and swooping close to the water. Her father often fondly watched from below as the two giggled with sheer pleasure at this blissful expression of their freedom.

Young Azuria was tender hearted, and kind to the woodland creatures. She

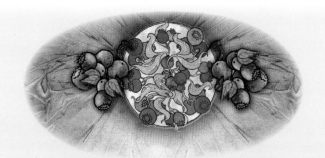

helped the neighborhood spider mothers keep track of their little ones — no easy task — and made friends with the squirrels who lived high up in the family dwellary. After she began flying on her own, Azuria made sure the roddeels had berry treats for their screeching chicks, whose hungry mouths were always open in expectation of food.

The berry fairy child wasn't perfect. Sehra sometimes lost patience with her daughter's daydreaming and farfetched notions. But it was not a serious complaint — creative daydreams and farfetched notions often lead to new and better methods of berry care and use. For example, there was the time Azuria put together a field watering system using the hollow stems of dandelions. It worked well with the blueberry plants that were close to lakes and streams and is still in use today. On the other hand, the blueberry scalp treatment she invented didn't work out quite as well. A number of blue haired berry fairies who had used Azuria's free samples expressed their annoyance to Sehra, who was thankful when the color finally wore off.

Undaunted by occasional failure, the optimistic young fairy thought of original ideas and recipes for the blueberries. Ellen Twinkle, Azuria's pretty, dark-haired cousin, spent many an afternoon with Azuria concocting new dishes. John, the adoring father, loyally smacked his lips and vowed he'd never tasted anything better after the girls cooked up some seaweed blueberry jam. It failed to jell, however, so they ended up with lumpy syrup instead. Ellen, who loved laughter, joked that it would make another good scalp treatment, which brought a chuckle from John. But when her mother found out they had used forty of her best ceramic jars in the experiment, Azuria and Ellen spent the afternoon pouring the lumpy syrup onto the compost heap and washing all the jars. The two girls wisely decided to play outside that afternoon to allow Sehra time to relax.

Berry Fairy Friends

When her day's chores were done, Azuria played with her friends, Merris Goldentree of the Salmonberry Fairy Clan and Frammie Woodwillow of the Cranberry Fairy Clan. Cousin Ellen kept the close-knit group laughing with her clever sense of humor. In the darkness of somnin winters, they would join hands and dance in the dark as the glow from their wings made pretty patterns in the snow.

Blessed with bravado and fearlessness, the girls had many adventures, sometimes escaping danger by a hair's breadth — especially Merris, or Merri as her friends called her, who was the daredevil of the group.

Once, the energetic salmonberry fairy was showing off her loop-the-loops over Eagle River, and dipped the toe of one dainty red sandal to draw a rippling line in the water.

"Watch me!" she yelled, giggling as the water tickled her toes. Distracted by the other girls' laughs and screams, she forgot to be careful. Her butterfly companion, Perriwink, hovered in horror as a shiny fish leapt from the stream, his snapping jaws catching Merri's red sandal! Screams of joy turned to fright as Merri struggled. She jerked free, but lost her shoe to the hungry fish, which caused her great dismay.

Frammie, a petite fairy with short hair and dark brown eyes ringed by fashionable eyeglasses, was fascinated with gadgets. She perched for hours on her mushroom chair, figuring out new ways to use broken parts of old washing machines or electric mixers found at the trezoran.

The Fae-Granda Coming of Age

At the age of twelve, Azuria began her apprenticeship as a Berry-Fairy-in-Training. It was the coming-of-age — the fae granda. She was leaving her childhood behind. Azuria would miss the happy, carefree times; no longer

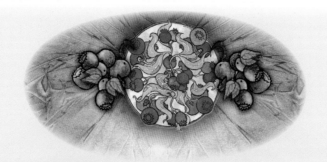

would she spend hours at play. Yet she was also looking forward with excitement to new, more adult activities, and to the tasks ahead that would call for her keen, creative mind and the strong work ethic that had been bred into her.

She joined Ellen, Merris and Frammie at the Fae Granda Ceremony, receiving her first magic konjor. Azuria would not only begin her regular berry fairy apprenticeship along with the other girls; she would also start fae-rejent training to prepare her for leadership of the clan.

In preparation for this momentous event, Sehra sewed a fae granda formal frock for Azuria. Made from soft blue rakneet silk, it had generous sleeves lined in pink satin, and a high Grecian waist and full skirt that twirled as Azuria excitedly spun to show it off. Sehra did the final fittings and declared it finished, and Azuria scooted to her closet to find shoes to wear with it. She decided on pale blue slippers studded with multicolored chanteel jewels; they were exactly the right choice. Her mother and father admired the fairy girl and whispered to each other how regal she looked.

Airith, the Dragonfly Ayonatta

Airith, Azuria's dragonfly companion, would be included in the ceremony; she would take an oath, swearing allegiance to her constant companion. The beautiful dragonfly would serve as Azuria's lifelong ayonatta, her most loyal, devoted friend and keeper of all her secrets.

Azuria Begins Her Training

Azuria's mother supervised her leadership training as well as her apprenticeship, which included lessons in camouflage techniques, orienteering, tool sharpening, transplanting, pruning and a host of other skills. Every few years she took exams with Queen Prasidea, who looked forward to reading Azuria's essays and inventive short stories. An avid reader, the young fairy earned extra credit by studying the ancient texts at the Berry Fairy Library. She was sought

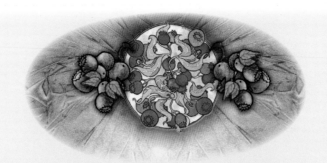

after by the other apprentices as a study group partner.

Azuria's favorite lessons were in the casting of magic spells. She quickly mastered simple ones using her new magic konjor and moved on to the intricate wrist movements for more complicated charms. She memorized the laws governing magic use, keeping her Berry Fairy Reference Manual of Magic handy at all times. Unlike magical practices in other fairy races, berry fairy magic is conservatively used because, with each use, it consumes a bit of the berry fairies' energy and life force. One who foolishly overuses magic for trivial tasks will have a shorter life span, and careless conjuring is considered wasteful. Each fairy, as she grows into her young womanhood, makes a decision about her magic use. Some want an easier, lazier life, overuse their magic, and take the consequence of a shorter one. Azuria's attitude on magic mirrored her mother's: practice regularly to become an expert, but never be wasteful.

The young blueberry fairy attended Berry Fairy Seminary on the Isle of Aeradeet, where the eldeera faculty taught berry fairy history, music, and astronomy. The eldeera also presided over annual spelling bees. In berry fairy spelling bees, unlike the shiltayen ones which are concerned with the spelling of words, the fairy girls refine their spell-casting expertise by competing at magic incantations such as changing the color of hats — *"Zeltin Creatisteen!"*— or conjuring toys for the little ones.

Grandmother Brittallo

Azuria adored her grandmother and visited her at least twice a week at her apartment on Aeradeet. The youngster enjoyed helping with chores and playing her violin in the Round House common room concerts.

Grandmother Brittallo taught her the old traditions of Alaska berry fairy global navigation using the stars, cloud formations and the northern lights.

They spent many happy hours in fields of fragrant clover, gazing up at the

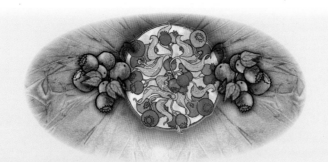

clouds. Azuria's favorite formation was the cirrus, or mare's tail clouds. Their gauzy, thin sweeps across the sky reminded her of pale lengths of rakneet silk. Cirrus clouds were of interest to most berry fairies since they often mean a change in weather, and affect flight patterns.

Grandmother Brittallo read berry fairy lore to Azuria from tattered books handed down by her own grandmother, and told fascinating stories about the Twinkle Clan. The best ones featured Sehra. Azuria loved hearing all about her mother's childhood adventures, both the good and the mischievous.

Success and Happiness

Thus, the decades passed; the natural rhythms of Alaska berry fairy life hummed in tune with nature as the berries continued to thrive. Azuria Blue Twinkle enjoyed her happy youth, working hard, making friendships that would last a lifetime, loving her family and exploring the northern realm that was her beloved home.

The Twinkle family seemed destined to continue guiding the Alaska Blueberry Fairy Clan to abundance and prosperity in Alaska, the Land of the Midnight Sun.

GLOSSARY OF NEKTFAHR WORDS
Berry fairies speak Nektfahr, a dialect of the fairy realms.

AYONATTA: *ay-on-NOT-ah.* Winged insect companion for a berry fairy.

BOREAL: *bor-ree-AL.* The private meditation chamber in every berry fairy's dwellary.

CHANTEEL: *chan-TEEL.* Berry fairy jewelry.

DEEYIN: *DEE-in.* Berry fairies that govern sweet, edible berries.

DWELLARY: *DWELL-a-ree.* Alaska berry fairy home.

ELDEERA: *eld-DEER-ra.* The berry fairy elders.

FAE-REJENT: *fay-REJ-jent.* The leader of a berry fairy clan.

FAE-GRANDA: *fay-GROND-ah.* Berry fairy coming-of-age ceremony.

FORESTFOLKE: *FOR-est-folk.* A short, elf-like male race with green hair, known for their kindness, charm and intelligence. They are handy, and can repair anything — a definite plus for the berry fairies. Although they cannot fly, they can leap great distances with the grace of leopards.

GLAYIN: *GLAY-in.* Fairies that govern poisonous or medicinal berries.

INVONDEE: *in-VON-dee.* Magic mist that conceals the Isle of Aeradeet.

JANEERA: *jan-EER-a.* A form of yoga-like exercise with meditation.

KRILLKLAW: *KRILL-klaw.* Magpie. *Not* berry fairy-friendly. Will stalk and devour them whenever possible.

KONJOR: *KON-jor.* Magic bracelet.

MYINZILL: *MY-in-zill.* Weather-resistant aura.

RAKNEET: *RAK-neet.* Spider web.

RENUVELLE: *ren-noo-VEL.* Spring time of the year.

RODDEEL: *rod-DEEL.* Raven; friend and protector of berry fairies.

SAKRE NINYIN: *SOK-ra-NIN-yin.* The Nine Sacred Principles that guide the lives of berry fairies.

SOMNIN: *SOM-nin.* Winter time.

TREZORAN: *trez-ZOR-in.* Shiltayen dump or landfill.

FACTS ABOUT ALASKA

ALASKA: *uh-LAS-ka.* Three miles from Russia, Alaska, the 49th state, is also known as the great land, the last frontier, and the land of the midnight sun. Larger than the next four biggest states together, it has more coastline than all the rest of the combined United States. There are over three million lakes in Alaska. There are more small airplanes per capita than in any other state. The U.S.A. purchased Alaska from Russia in 1867 for $7.2 million.

ALASKAN TUXEDO: *uh-LAS -kan tux-EE-doe.* A sturdy, warm woolen suit, commonly a twill weave in dark olive green, often worn with a casual shirt and string tie.

ANCHORAGE: *ANK-or-aj.* Half of Alaska's population lives there. It is a modern city with professional sports teams, TV and radio stations, an international airport and universities. Culturally it is rich, with an array of native arts as well as opera, symphony, visual and performing arts. Anchorage has been honored with the title of "All America City" four times.

ANTLERS: *ANT-lerz.* Antlers grow in spring, and have a soft covering known as velvet which drops off later. They are shed yearly in fall (unlike horns, which begin at birth and grow until the animal dies. Horns are not shed). A moose's antlers can be four or five feet wide.

COOK INLET: *cook IN-lit.* A body of water in Southcentral Alaska measuring 180 miles from the Gulf of Alaska to Anchorage. Turnagain Arm and Knik Arm both connect to Cook Inlet.

KENAI PENINSULA: *KEEN-eye pen-IN-sul-a.* The peninsula south of Anchorage. To drive down the Kenai, you must travel all the way around Turnagain Arm on the Seward Highway. There are many mountains, glaciers and lakes on the Kenai, along with towns such as Kenai, Soldotna, Seward, Homer, Sterling (formerly known as Naptown) and Seldovia.

KODIAK BEAR: *KOD-ee-ak bair.* The largest bears in the world live on Kodiak Island; they can reach over ten feet tall on their hind legs. There are only about 3500 in existence. They eat all kinds of food and love berries. Never go near a bear because they sometimes eat people too.

KODIAK ISLAND: *KOD-ee-ak EYE-land.* Kodiak,100 miles long and 60 miles wide at some spots, is the second largest island in the U.S. A large Coast Guard force is maintained there to serve and protect the many miles of Alaska's coast.

MATANUSKA VALLEY: *MAT-ah-NOOS-ka VAL-lee.* Also called the Mat Su Valley, from the Matanuska and Susitna Rivers in southcentral Alaska. it is known for its rugged mountain beauty, sparkling lakes and verdant forests. Gold is mined in the mountains that border the area. Cities include Knik, Wasilla, Palmer, Houston, Big Lake, Willow and Talkeetna.

MOOSE: *moos.* Members of the deer family, Alaska's moose are the biggest of those anywhere. Colors can be toasty tan or light brownish black. Moose hair is hollow which insulates their bodies. Stiff, coarser hair grows on the hump on their backs. If you see a moose with its ears laid back and its back hair raised, it is nervous or angry. Best to avoid them in any case.

QUONSET: *KWON-set.* Pre-fabricated shelter consisting of a semi-circular rib structure covered with corrugated sheet metal, commonly used in Alaska starting in WW II.

SOURDOUGH: *SOUW-er doe.* Bread made by California miners during the Gold Rush. It was brought to Alaska during the Klondike Gold Rush and carried next to the body to keep it warm. A long-time Alaskan is also called a sourdough.

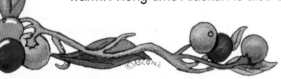

A-2

*BERRIES MENTIONED IN THIS BOOK

BEARBERRIES: The botanical name for bearberries means "bear grapes." Bears greatly enjoy this fruit, which varies from purple to red in color. The leaves are used in herbal medicine.

BLUEBERRIES: There are many types of blueberries. They are favorites of people and animals alike. Declared a "super food" by some health experts, they are a great sources of Vitamin C and other healthy substances. Some think they reverse the effects of aging. Delicious in pancakes, jam, jelly, porridge, milkshakes, or just eaten out of hand.

CRANBERRIES: Both highbush (pictured) and lowbush are picked in Alaska. Highbush: the bushes can be four feet tall and have a distinctive aroma and red fruit. Lowbush: Bright red fruit, smaller than highbush with small shiny leaves. Both kinds of these tart berries benefit from adding sweetener.

DEVIL'S CLUB: A tall plant with sharp thorns on the stalks and the undersides of the giant leaves. They produce clusters of oval, orange-red berries. Native cultures are said to use it to ease pain or disease ranging from headaches to arthritis and diabetes. This plant is graceful, stately and beautiful (from a safe distance; the thorns can penetrate tough denim).

SALMONBERRIES: The salmonberry, a juicy fruit ranging from salmon pink to red, grows in a cluster formation. They have a delicate flavor and are delicious eaten from the plant, or in jams and jellies.

SNOWBERRIES: Mildly toxic to children, they may be fatal to animals. These white berries are not only decorative, but useful. They are used as shampoo and when the fruit and leaves are crushed, they can be applied to cuts as a poultice. In olden tiimes, the bark was used in tea to treat tuberculosis.

*Don't eat berries unless you are certain they are edible! For more information, explore your library or the internet. Verna Pratt has written several helpful books on flowers and berries that grow in Alaska. Find her books at www.alaskakrafts.com.